Dropwort Hall

A Magical Tale

Written and illustrated

by

Kathy Sharp

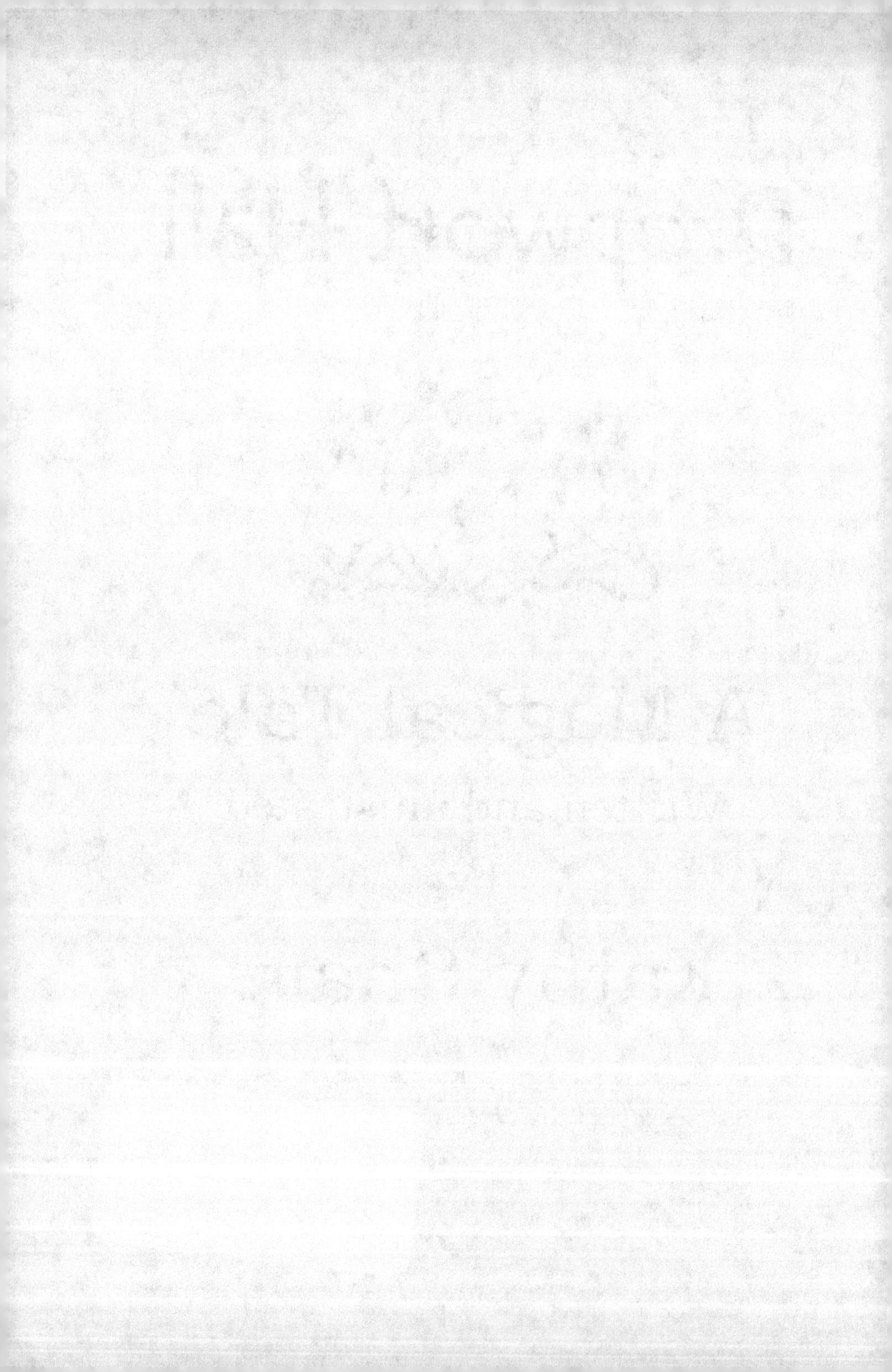

VENEFICIA PUBLICATIONS UK

veneficiapublications.com
veneficiapublications@gmail.com

Typesetting © Veneficia Publications
UK October 2021

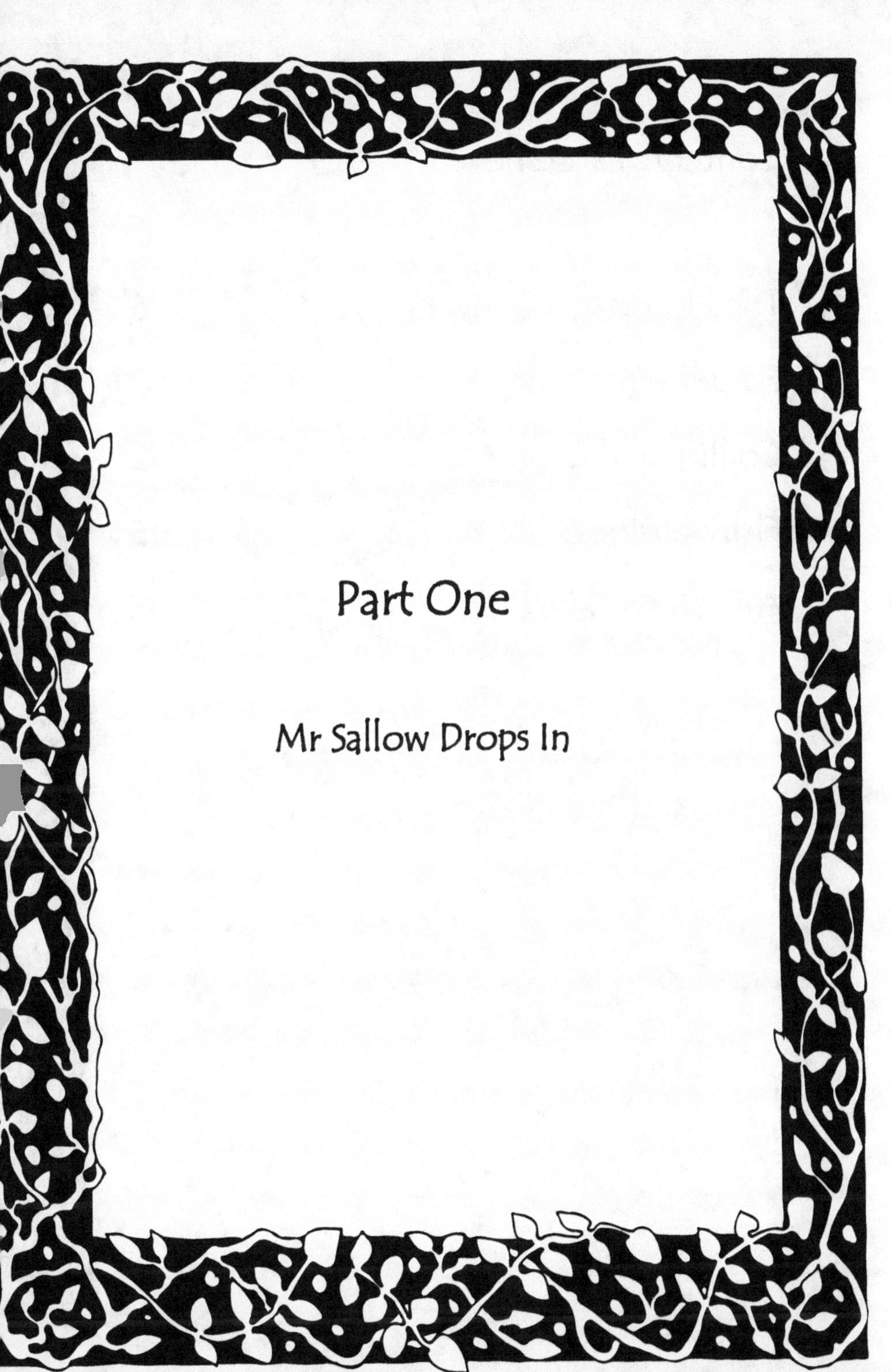

Part One

Mr Sallow Drops In

Contents Part One

The House by the River

Inspired by the Grey Sallow (*Salix cinerea*) an unassuming, common waterside tree whose roots help to secure riverbanks.

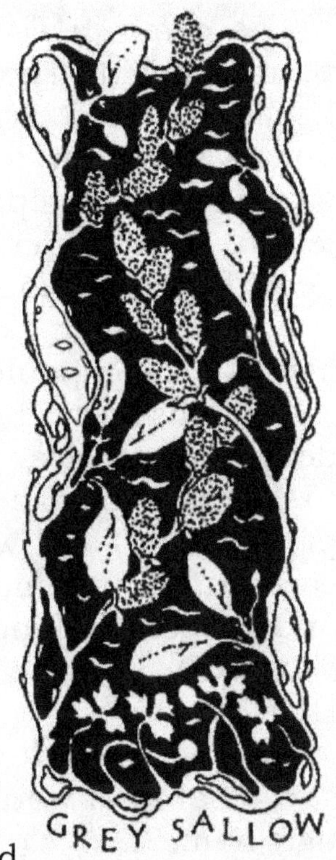

Mr Sallow picked his way along the edge of the water meadows. He stopped, shifted the bundle he carried on his back, looked with interest at the great house on the riverbank and moved on. Not the best time of year to be in such a place, with the stream full to bursting, and indeed, completely burst here and there. The banks had not been well-maintained, he thought, as he cast a waterman's eye over the scene. Some of the little weirs were broken down, the ditches left to fill with silt; it needed proper management. He looked again towards the house, pursed his lips, and shaded his eyes. He could just make out the end of the long wall, covered heavily by ivy; its stonework eroded by weather and roots, every bit as neglected as the water-meadows and weirs. The place seemed in a state of advanced and possibly permanent slumber.

'Well,' he said to nobody in particular, 'high time it was woken up, I'd say,' and he trudged on through the mud, with a distinctly determined step.

As he came in sight of the unkempt gateway, he paused again. The bundle on his back unwound itself, acquired arms and legs, and, shimmying downwards, put out a fastidious toe to the cold ground before stepping down. An ape, in a woollen jerkin with antler buttons, and wearing a very doubtful expression.

Mr Sallow looked affectionately into the wise face of his companion and said,

'This house here is a blank sheet, Crowfoot my dear. A clean, clear blank space ready for me, for us, to take in hand. The people here are waiting for us, I promise you, and we shall not be turned away.' He gazed up at the many gables, taking in broken tiles and suspect-looking windowsills.

'Oh, and the name of the house is Dropwort Hall.'

The ape looked up, raising an eyebrow, as if to say, what idiot would give a grand building such an ugly name?

Mr Sallow shook his head, understanding perfectly.

'It is a good name, and an ancient one. Sometimes people call it Drop-dead Hall, you know.' The ape sniggered. 'Yes, yes, Crowfoot, laugh if you will, but it's a house that has changed owners so many times after sudden deaths, that it has thoroughly earned that name. And if my information is correct, which I'm sure it is, the curse of the house – for people do say it's a curse – has lately struck once again, and there is a grieving widow left alone here.' The ape looked solemn. 'Yes, it is tragic, Crowfoot, but it is also an opportunity. For us.'

The ape raised an enquiring eyebrow again.

'Oh, no, my dear,' said Mr Sallow, 'the curse will not affect us. It strikes the owner, not the hired help. Have no fear at all. The house needs our help – look at the state of the mullions. It is ailing. It will never harm us. The window of opportunity is left ajar for us, and we need do nothing but climb in through it. So, come along now.'

The ape shrugged, took Mr Sallow's proffered hand, and ambled with him along the ruined riverbank towards the house, which seemed not only to have awakened, but to be holding its breath in anticipation.

The Lady of the House

Inspired by the Sweet Cicely (*Myrrhis odorata*), an old-fashioned, widely grown herb, scented with aniseed.

The widow looked him up and down.

'I am mistress Cicely,' she said.

Mr Sallow bowed.

'Your servant, ma'am. And your namesake is by the kitchen door. '

'What?' she said, confused. 'The kitchen ...'

Mr Sallow smiled.

'Why, Sweet Cicely, ma'am. The herb. And a very good herb; your cook will use it to sweeten a dish of cooked medlars. I see you have a tree in the garden.'

He looked around at the sadly scruffy wood panelling.

'And I have another use for it, I see.'

He said no more, and the widow looked at him sideways.

'Does wonders rubbed into a bit of oak,' said Mr Sallow.

The room, high-ceilinged, smelt of smoke.

'Something amiss with your chimneys, ma'am,' he said mildly. 'I may be able to help. There's a real art in getting the fires to work prop'ly, y'know. Been neglected, have they?'

There was no need for this gentle question, not really. There were signs of neglect everywhere. They were written all over her face, too.

'Since my husband died ...' she said. It was enough.

'Ah,' said Mr Sallow. And that was enough too. 'I was looking at the weirs as I came past. Sad to see things in disrepair, isn't it?'

He suspected it wasn't lack of money that was causing the dilapidation. His careful eye had noted the displacement of stone tiles on the porch roof, with tell-tale runnels of rainwater. No, not lack of money, just of will, and some sort of organisation. The house and its environs had become sad along with the widow. There was a crying need for someone to manage this little estate.

But would she trust him if he offered to take it on? A complete stranger? And could he trust her if she agreed to anything so foolish? That was a serious conundrum, and he warmed his hands at the sputtering fire while he considered it. The widow waited in silence as if she had read his thoughts.

At last, he stood back.

'Why don't I just start with the fires, ma'am? Get them drawing prop'ly. It'll make everything more comfortable; don't you think?'

And it began just as easily as that.

A Clean and Silent Creature

Inspired by Water Crowfoot (*Ranunculus penicillatus*) a plant of fast-flowing streams.

'I haven't let a priest through these doors since my husband died,' said the widow apropos of nothing. She wasn't sure why she found Mr Sallow so easy to talk to, but it was a considerable relief when she had felt so alone.

'Trying to make people confess their sins on their deathbed is plain wrong.

Anyone in that situation is busy enough without being made to take the blame for the past.'

Mr Sallow nodded in agreement.

'It is a dubious benefit, Mistress Cicely.' he said. 'If I have transgressed, which like any mortal I do from time to time, I simply confess all to Master Crowfoot here.' He looked fondly at the ape at his side. 'He listens to everything, repeats nothing and judges not at all, which is more than you can say for the priesthood.'

The ape assumed an expression of silent wisdom and folded his hands over his jerkin.

The widow had been taken aback at first by the ape. You didn't see many of them, not in

Dorsetshire. An ape in a jerkin, with antler buttons. Mr Sallow doted on the animal, and it was sometimes difficult to tell who the owner was and who was the pet. Their features often took on the same expression, and if the ape could only speak, the widow thought, it would sometimes finish Mr Sallow's sentences for him.

The two of them had arrived with the rain, dribbled in, the most damp and bedraggled pair the widow had ever seen, and she had seen some bedraggled people in her time. But thanks to Mr Sallow's astonishing powers of fixing things, they had settled quite naturally as part of the household. Crowfoot the Ape was a thoroughly clean animal, most fastidious in his personal habits; more particular than some of the servants, for sure. So, beyond a few rudimentary raisings of eyebrows, no-one had questioned his inclusion.

And on the whole, the widow thought, confessing your sins to this clean and silent creature was preferable to bringing in the clergy. Some of them had dirty habits.

He was an exceptionally ugly man, the widow thought, but that could be easily forgiven when you made yourself as thoroughly useful as Mr Sallow did. He had begun with the many chimneys, large and small, and now every one of them was clean and efficient. She had no idea how he had done it, but it hardly mattered. If he had waved a magic wand or made a pact with the devil, she didn't care. He seemed to have expertise in all practical matters. The servants worked willingly for him in a way they never had for her. The shouting and petty theft in the kitchens had mostly ceased.

She had paid him a small, steady wage, and he hadn't quibbled or tried to bargain for more. She had handed over the nearly ruinous stable block for his own use, and he had swiftly turned it into not only living quarters for himself, but an efficient estate-office, too. And there was still room for horses should she need to accommodate any.

Tomorrow, he told her cheerfully, he would begin on mending the weirs and sorting out the fishing-rights to the stream, both badly neglected. The thought trembled in Mistress Cicely's mind that she should be more suspicious of his motives. After all, you could say that he was taking over the estate one aspect at a time, or that he was making decisions above his station, and might already have his fingers in the coffers. However, neither she, her servants nor anyone on the estate ever suspected him of any wrongdoing. He seemed to be that very rare bird, a completely honest man.

Mr Sallow came to her rescue the day the widow ruined her best gown. Green satin. The wide, graceful sleeve had been caught in a door, bad enough in itself, and then mangled in the newly oiled hinge, ending up torn and greased. Her struggles to disentangle it had made matters worse, not least when her skirt was drawn under the door and had torn on the rough edge of the iron sill. She was in tears of fury when Mr Sallow came in.

'Deliver the gown and sleeves to me, ma'am, and I'll have them back to you in a trice, good as new.'

And so, he did. The gown was returned invisibly mended, grease free and without so much as a crimp from the mangling in the hinge.

'No-one could know all these things,' she said. 'You repaired the chimneys in a most expert way. You mended the weirs to perfection. You removed all that ivy with no damage at all to the mortar in the walls. You have made every paving stone in the hall that I've been tripping over for years perfectly even. You cured two sheep of the moping sickness against all odds, you have stopped the servants from stealing the cheese, and many other useful things. No-one but a sorcerer could achieve so much in so little time.'

'I am an industrious person, ma'am,' said Mr Sallow, taking no umbrage at all at the casual accusation of sorcery. 'I learn from people wherever I go – and incidentally, I have smoothed the iron sills of the doors to avoid further damage to your gowns, and I am inventing a non-mangling hinge. Oh, and I have cured the galloping blight on your apple trees, too.'

Forget-me-not

Inspired by the Water Forget-Me-Not (*Myosotis scorpioides*), often used as a symbol of lost love.

The widow stood before the portrait of her late husband, looking at it quizzically. Not a very good likeness, not really. She wondered if the court painter kept a stock of ready-made portraits, ready to add a few pertinent details to each to suit the sitter. Richard had been a lawyer, a minor dignitary at court, and probably not deserving of any sort of made-to-measure portrait. That was probably why he appeared to be wearing a false nose. A distinguishing feature added as an afterthought to a stock painting. Poor quality paint, poor quality workmanship. She supposed the portrait would confer immortality of a kind on her husband; a permanent reminder of him. But in all honesty, she thought, Crowfoot the Ape could have painted a better one. Right on cue, the ape put his neat head round the door, took in the situation, and sidled over. He regarded the painting for a few moments then looked up into her face. She raised an eyebrow;

the ape glanced again at the picture and shook his head minutely. Not only a confessor, then, but a considerable art critic, too, she thought. An ape of excellent good taste. That could only be a useful item to have about the house, for sure.

Codlins and Cream

Inspired by the Great Willowherb (*Epilobium hirsutum*), a common plant of the riverbank, also known as codlins (apples) and cream, referring to its pink and white flowers.

Mr Sallow's most inventive creation followed a complaint on the part of the widow that food invariably ran cold between the kitchens and the solar upstairs, where she chose to eat it. He could have suggested, of course, that she eat downstairs in the hall, as was customary, closer to the kitchens. But he knew the solar was better lit – the widow's eyes not being as good they once were. Of course, she preferred to dine upstairs.

'Ma'am,' he said, 'I believe I can solve the problem.'

Mistress Cicely the widow looked doubtful. Unless he could magic the dishes direct from kitchen to solar, how was it to be done? But she had learned that it was unwise to underestimate Mr Sallow's ingenuity. She shrugged and left him to it.

So, Mr Sallow and his associate, Crowfoot the Ape, set to work. There was a great sound of sawing and hammering from the lean-to workshop near the kitchen door, and the widow noted a slight seasoning of sawdust on her meals. But there was no real disruption. Whatever Mr Sallow had in mind proceeded in an untroublesome way, some of it at night, when the widow had retired to her distant room in the east wing.

One morning Mr Sallow appeared before her and bowed, Crowfoot the Ape beside him, solemnly bowing, too. The effect was so comical that the widow cracked a rare smile.

'Mr Sallow,' she said, 'and, er, Master Crowfoot.' The pair regarded her a moment, glanced at each other and then Mr Sallow made a follow-me-if-you-please gesture and all three proceeded to the solar.

The widow peered around.

'There is no difference,' she said, disappointed.

Mr Sallow bowed again.

'Exactly, ma'am. Crowfoot, if you would?' and the ape hopped over to the wood panelling and put his bony thumb to a specific corner of the linenfold. There was a soft click and the panel retreated, sliding neatly behind its neighbour. Revealed was a tiny, perfect spiral staircase.

'Crowfoot?' said Mr Sallow again, and the ape straightened his jerkin and hopped onto the staircase, heading down. Mr Sallow folded his hands and waited in silence. Very soon the ape reappeared up the stairs, taking them two at a time balanced upside down on his hairy knuckles and bearing a dish of hot baked apples and cream aloft in his equally hairy feet.

'Stop showing off,' said Mr Sallow, taking the dish and handing it to the widow. 'Now, will that do, ma'am?'

The widow tasted. Very good. Very hot.

'Remarkable!' she said. 'But how...?'

'The stairs connect directly with the kitchens,' said Mr Sallow.

'It is but a hop, skip and a jump for your serving maids to bring your dinner to the table all hot.' He pressed the panel again, so the door closed. 'And the beauty of your panelling is not disturbed at all.'

The ape, unable to contain itself any longer took a flying leap into the rafters and swung from one to another, whooping with delight.

'Get down here and behave yourself, Crowfoot,' said Mr Sallow sternly. 'My apologies, ma'am, but he's pleased with his handiwork.'

The ape landed on the floor with a plop and resuming his solemn expression, secretly wiped his hands on the back of the widow's skirts as he rejoined his master. The pair bowed in unison and retreated, sharing a knowing glance.

Fishy Business

Inspired by the Yellow Waterlily (*Nuphar lutea*), a plant of slow-running or still water, like fishponds.

YELLOW WATERLILY

Although the landscape slept through the worst of the winter, the little river did not. It grew a rack of ice along its margins and rushed and rattled along keeping the centre of the stream clear. Mr Sallow went out and crunched through the frosty grass, taking depth markings with a long stick, and nodding wisely as he went. He seemed at home with the river, and was on cordial terms with it, chatting as he went, making practical suggestions for its better future.

Mistress Cicely, the widow, watched at a window, thinking the river would take his advice if it had any sense. Mr Sallow always seemed to know best. He wanted to dig a fish-pool in the marshy ground, and when he had put the suggestion to her, the widow agreed and came away thinking it had been her own excellent idea. She had no notion of how he'd managed that when she thought about it later. All Mr Sallow's ideas were sound, but he was careful to let the widow herself own them. That was his particular genius.

He had marked out the boundaries for the pool with stakes before he had even suggested it to her. He had estimated the increase in fish available to the kitchens, in case anyone should ask, and could quote the benefits told him by an abbot who had dug a similar pond in a nearby monastery. A stock of fish was already on order. He had organised a gang of diggers ready to start work as soon as ever the frost came out of the ground. Mr Sallow always got his own way.

When the river flooded there was an emergency in the nether world of the cellars, too. Once again, Mr Sallow was on hand straight away to organise the rescue of cheeses and hams, onions, and turnips. However, Crowfoot the Ape, who had no business to be in the cellars was carried out clutching an almost empty bottle of the late master's fine wine.

In the kitchen, only inches above the fateful water-level, Mr Sallow kept the fires burning, magicking dry logs out of God-knows-where when everything was sodden. And it was Mr Sallow who set the whole topsy-turvy place back in order when the waters retreated.

'There,' he said, when all was clean and cleared, 'my fish pool will act as an overflow, and the diggings from it will form a levee on the riverbank too. We'll have no more flooding.'

The widow pursed her lips, noting the use of 'my' fish pool. It was a rare slip, on Mr Sallow's part, and he caught the expression on her face and knew directly what had put it there.

'Your fish pool will prevent flooding ma'am,' he said in his measured way. But the damage was done. The widow nodded her agreement, but he noted the sideways look she gave him as he left the room.

'And keep that damnable ape out of the cellars,' she called after him. It was the first order she had ever given him.

A Rush to Take Over

Inspired by the Soft Rush (*Juncus effusus*), a common and useful plant of damp places.

Ever since the widow had lost her husband, things had fallen into disrepair and disarray. No-one was happy in contemplating an ever more dishevelled future, in which both the fabric and the atmosphere of the house – not to mention its wider reputation – would collapse into ruin.

So, the arrival of the able and organised Mr Sallow had pleased everyone, even if it had all happened in something of a rush. And there had been no complaints at all while he set the household, and the estate, to rights.

Everything was running like clockwork, everything in good repair and good order, and the house had shaken off its air of dishevelment; the servants were properly and promptly paid, and the estate would generate wealth in the coming year. However, people had begun to talk, to ask awkward questions, and to seek reasons to be annoyed.

Mr Sallow had anticipated this change and remarked mildly to Mistress Cicely that people always needed something to fret about.

'When their living is not in danger,' he said, 'when things are settled, and when everyone has most of what they need in life, you can be sure they will turn on any benefactor. Bite the hand that feeds them, as they say.'

The widow had turned to him in alarm at this forecast of gross ingratitude.

'Do you mean they will bite my hand, Mr Sallow?'

'Oh, no, ma'am,' he said. 'I am here to fulfil that function. But do not be surprised if you hear strange tales about me. I have set things in order for them – and, believe me, no such good deed can go unpunished. I can only beg that you bear it in mind when the gossip starts, as it surely will.'

The gossip, of course, was keeping good time and had already begun.

'What do you make of 'im?' asked the butler, peering out of the pantry window. The cook shrugged.

'Them as soars too high gets singed by the sun, sir,' she said. 'Too much altitude will bring its own punishment, I reckon.'

They stood together, watching as Mr Sallow climbed to the very top of the dovecot roof. He had his eye on a slipped and broken tile, with Crowfoot the Ape bearing a bag of tools lolloping up after him.

'That ape is a great help to 'im,' observed the butler.

'That's true,' said the cook, watching as Crowfoot overtook his master and settled on the carved wooden pinnacle at the top, holding on with his flexible toes. This left both hands free to fish spare roof-tiles and tools out of the bag.

'But there's some that say he's not a natural animal – that he understands what we say.'

The butler scratched his nose, thinking.

'He seems to understand what that Sallow-fellow says. But any dog or horse will become accustomed to the voice of his master – it don't mean anything unnatural.'

'Oh, I know that' said the cook, airily. 'Course I do. But I've heard him ask that animal's advice. With my own ears, sir.'

'Didn't get a reply, did he?' said the butler, sniggering.

'Not such as you or I could make sense of no. That ape contorts its face and flicks its furry eyebrows, and that Mr Sallow nods to it just as if it had said something. It's not right.'

'So, what do you think it is, then?' said the butler.

'I know nothing, sir. And I don't speculate, neither. But I do hear tell of witches – witches that has unnatural animals – demons in animal form – that run alongside them and do magical things. And those witches talk to them, just like Mr Sallow does to that there ape.'

The butler looked mildly shocked.

'Are you suggesting that ape is a familiar?'

'I suggest nothing, sir,' said the cook quickly. 'But people do talk.' She withdrew, satisfied that she had spread such a juicy piece of gossip while distancing herself from the source (actually, the under-gardener who resented the extra work Mr Sallow had caused him, and was thus not a very reliable witness).

But any finger-pointing in the witchcraft line was very dangerous stuff. And that, of course, made it completely irresistible.

Despite these unhelpful scraps of gossip, the benignly regimented life of Dropwort Hall had moved smoothly along in a pleasingly clockwork fashion for almost half a year. The household was ticking over nicely to the collection of legislation – all of it entirely logical and reasonable – that Mr Sallow imposed upon it. The widow blessed the day chance had brought him and Crowfoot the Ape to her door. She turned a blind eye to the ape's occasional peculiar habits and ignored snide suggestions that Mr Sallow might be attempting to take over the place by subterfuge. And most people agreed with her – right up to the day the first death occurred.

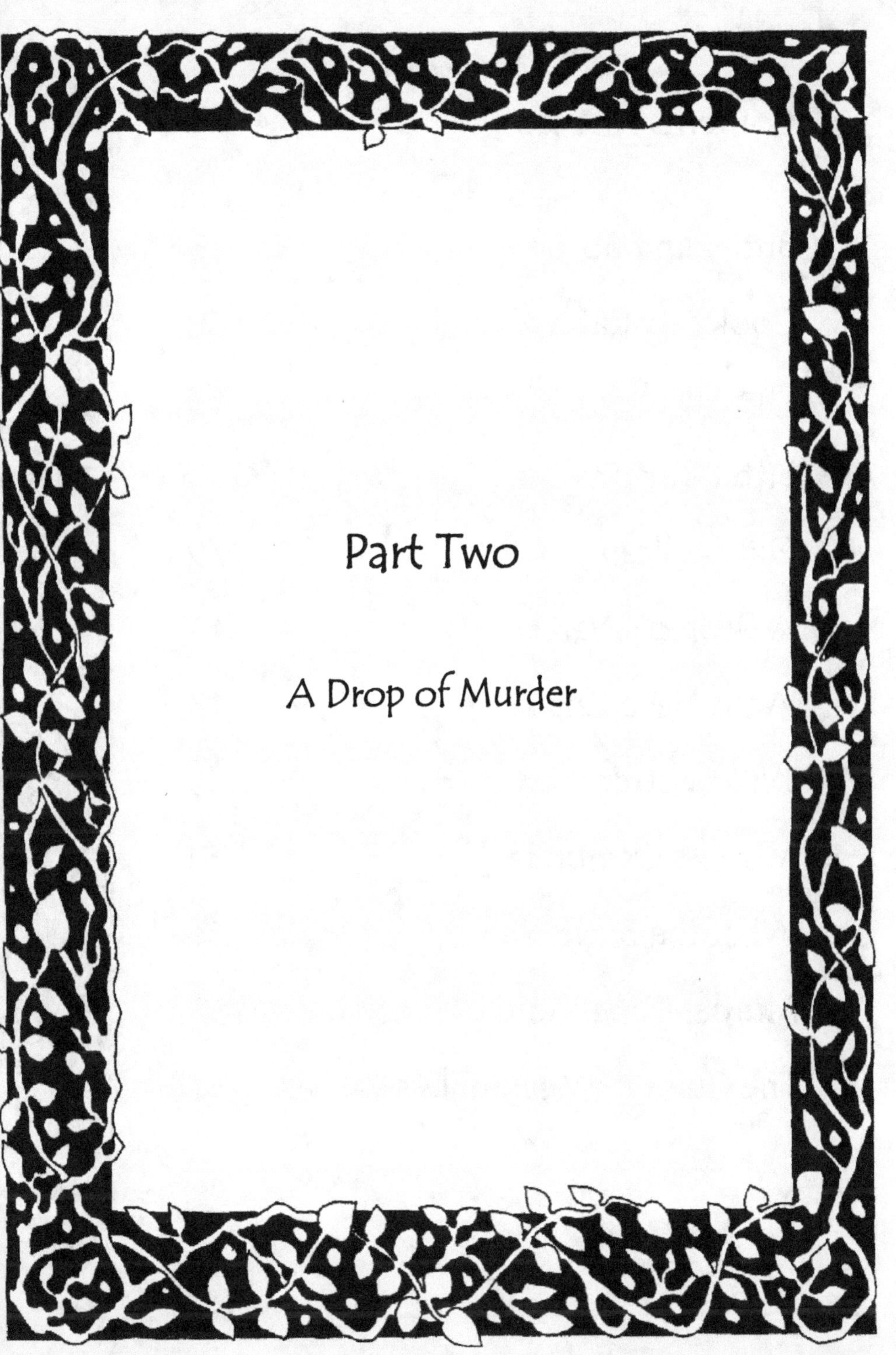# Part Two

A Drop of Murder

Contents Part Two

Butler and Bottle

Inspired by the Bottle Sedge
(*Carex rostrata*) a plant of
marshy places, so called
because the seeds resemble
long-necked bottles.

The widow, even in the
most distant part of the house,
clearly heard the shout. So did
just about everyone else. Mr
Sallow, alarmed at any danger of
interruption to the smooth
running of the household,
including any unregulated
shouting, ran in and grabbed the
boot-boy by the scruff of the neck,
demanding to know where the trouble
was.

'Wine cellar, y'honour,' said the boy instantly.
He was never quite sure how to address Mr Sallow,
seeing as he seemed to be neither quite upstairs nor
downstairs.

Soon, though, he was definitely downstairs.
The butler had been found collapsed in a pool of
blood.

'Could be forgiven for shouting, then,'
somebody observed, 'under the circumstances.'

People were gathering at the cellar door,
craning their necks for a good look, but reluctant to
enter. Mr Sallow shooed them all back.

'I shall deal with this,' he said, though there was an edge of worry in his usual confident tone. This too could be forgiven under the circumstances. 'Come with me please,' Mr Sallow said to the boot-boy, 'in case I require assistance.'

'Or a witness,' as somebody else observed. The butler was lying very still indeed and had completely ceased shouting. The cellar was as quiet as the grave.

Mr Sallow and his witness proceeded into the cellar and slammed the door in all the other expectant and curious faces. People listened at the door, of course, but in the absence of further information began to speculate. The kitchen maid said the butler had been stabbed through the heart with his own corkscrew and served the grumpy old fool right. When the widow came down at last to investigate all the fuss; the cook told her the butler had been bludgeoned with a cheese platter. Although, there was no evidence of this. The widow asked whether it was certain the poor man was actually dead at all.

'Oh, madam', they all said, 'such a puddle of blood! He must be dead for sure. Mr Sallow is in there with him.' The widow hesitated a moment with her hand on the door handle – she was perfectly entitled to enter her own wine-cellar if she so wished. Perhaps, she thought, it was better to leave it to Mr Sallow.

Mr Sallow's investigations, meanwhile, had ascertained that the pool of blood was in fact the late master's best Burgundy, the bottle having broken when the butler fell. The neck of the bottle was still in the man's hand. The boot-boy looked on warily.

'There is no wound, Mr Sallow, is there?' he said, very hushed. Mr Sallow shook his head, knelt in the puddle of wine, and sought a pulse, or a heartbeat but found none. However, it had happened, the butler was most definitely as dead as a doornail.

The late master of the house, as well as amassing a fine collection of doomed Burgundy, had been a lawyer, and had dealt with petty crime himself. His judgements had generally been reckoned as good enough, since he didn't go in for excessive punishment. However, an unexplained death, with or without shouting, was quite a different matter, and the boot boy had been sent out of the cellar to inform the widow that Mr Sallow recommended summoning a constable.

Speculation continued, however, and the curse of Dropwort Hall was cited.

It had taken the life of the poor late master, had it not, and made a widow of his good wife?

Some said the curse could only affect the owner, and butlers, definitely didn't count. Others said it was good, old-fashioned, black magic at work, as it had down the generations. No murder at all, just magic.

The constable, when they finally found him sober, did not agree, despite being side-tracked by the smell of the strong wine.

'Clean it up,' he said, 'and clean him up', indicating the deceased, 'and send for the priest.'

When interviews were held, hand on Bible, everyone swore they had heard the butler shout. And everyone swore they had seen nothing else. Except young Master Buttons, the under-gardener. He swore he had been at one of the little windows that formed all the light in the wine-cellar, peeking in with a view to helping himself to an illicit pot of ale if the coast were clear. No, he had not taken any ale, the coast not being clear with the butler there.

'But I did hear the butler shout, and I saw him fall, too, bottle and all.' The boy paused for effect. 'And I'll tell you something else, sir, I saw a shadow on the back wall. A shadow with prodigious long arms, it was.'

Mr Sallow became even paler than usual. Where exactly had Crowfoot, the Ape been at the time?

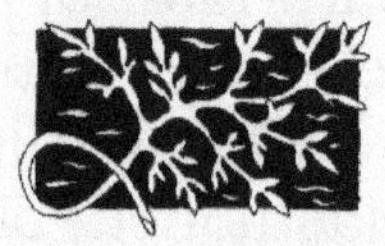

Cook and Cat

Inspired by the Reed Mace (*Typha latifolia*), a striking plant found in watery places, also called cattail.

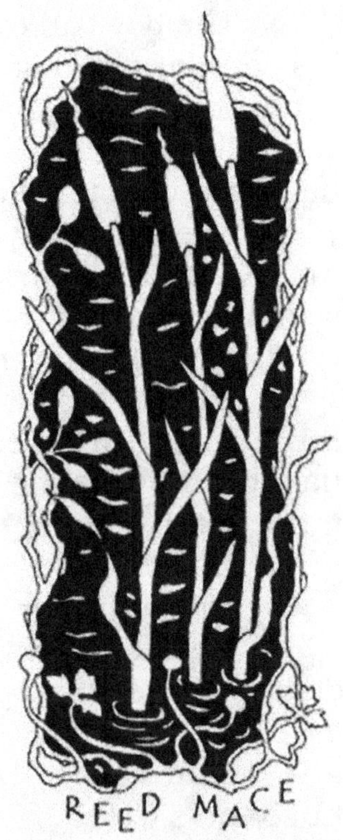

There was a good deal of gossip in the following days, and many a person appointed themselves judge and jury, saying they had never trusted that ape, no not ever.

Poor Crowfoot, clearly cracking under the strain of the accusing looks cast in his direction, made himself scarce, while Mr Sallow made painstaking investigations.

Things became much, much worse when the cook was found in the cellar, as dead as dead could be.

'Slumped, she was,' said the under-gardener, who seemed to have a real talent for being on the scene of foul play. 'Slumped on the chair, ladle full of wine still in her hand. I thought she'd had too much and fallen asleep, so I crept up and thumped her on the back. To give her a fright, dozy old besom. But she slid off the stool, straight to the floor. And I saw she weren't asleep at all. Good thing she's used to the heat, I thought. Gone on to a much hotter place!'

The boy ran out, with the kitchen maid boxing his ears for speaking ill of the dead.

'Touch nothing!' said Mr Sallow, looking carefully at the undisturbed scene before the harassed constable arrived once again.

Suspicious eyes were cast upon Crowfoot the Ape, who had followed Mr Sallow to the cellar and was now clinging to his master's shins in terror.

Mr Sallow read their minds.

'No-one has suggested that Crowfoot was in the vicinity during either of these deaths. Indeed, he has been with me all day. I can vouch for his innocence.'

'So, you say,' somebody muttered.

Mr Sallow ignored this.

'Besides,' he said, 'the common factor in these deaths is the wine, present by the puddleful in both cases.

'How dare you cast aspersions on my husband's wine!' said the widow. 'How dare you! It is the finest of its kind – from the king's own vintner. He was so proud of it ...' She trailed off, dabbing her eyes.

'I will look into it, ma'am,' said Mr Sallow, unfazed.

But he noted people still looking daggers at Crowfoot.

The widow was deeply embarrassed at having both the law and then the priest called to the premises again.

'Something must be done,' she said to Mr Sallow, when these unwelcome visitors had gone, and was about to deliver an ultimatum when further bad news was delivered.

The kitchen cat, according to several witnesses had mewed loudly, rolled over onto its back, paws in the air, and given up the ghost. Some said, of course, that a dead cat did not require an inquest, only a shovel. But Mr Sallow insisted upon a full investigation yet again.

The unexplained deaths of the butler and the cook were making everyone nervous, what with the house being under a curse. Every member of the household was keen to assess the degree of risk to themselves. The fate of the feline might befall any one of them, whatever the cause, be it magic or murder. Some said they couldn't see the curse stretching as far as the kitchen cat; no curse was that elastic, surely.

Mr Sallow tended to agree and said so. The curse, assuming it existed at all, applied to the master of the house alone. These incidents of household staff, and domestic animals dropping dead were unlikely to be magical in origin. However, something was causing them, and Mr Sallow meant to find out what it was.

However, the late master, people pointed out, had died of the curse, God bless his poor immortal soul. Dead as a doornail. Just like that there cat. This comment resulted in an extended argument as to whether the late cat possessed an immortal soul or not. And one or two queries about the late master, to boot.

Mr Sallow left them to it, looked around carefully, and then took the deceased away for closer examination, his mind working furiously.

'I wonder,' he muttered, 'I wonder ...' Crowfoot followed the corpse at a respectful distance, as if death might be catching, and disappeared up a tree when they stepped outside. Crowfoot, clearly deciding discretion was the better part of valour. Mr Sallow, absorbed in his theories, walked on, pausing only to sniff the cat and then stare into the distance awhile, still muttering 'I wonder ...'

The Madness of Crowfoot

Inspired by the Water Plantain (*Alisma plantago-aquatica*), once thought to be a cure for rabies.

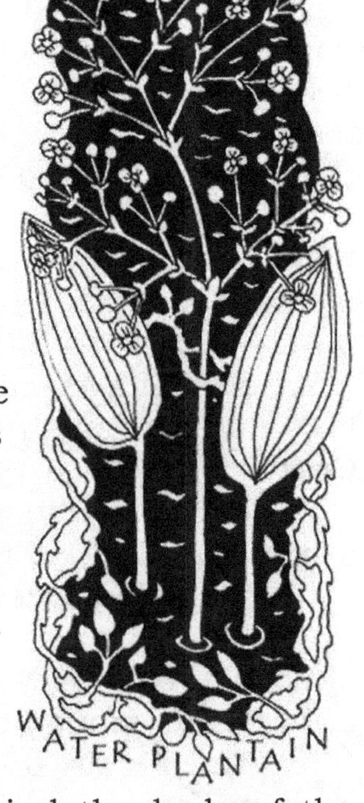

Mr Sallow was dismayed that suspicion should fall upon Crowfoot the Ape. He had never known his companion of many years to injure anyone. Apart from the occasional wild rampage through the treetops, or the rafters, the ape was a model of good behaviour, and often very kind in an animal sort of way. But the mysterious long-armed shadow, seen on the wall behind the body of the butler, preyed on Mr Sallow's mind. Could Crowfoot really have gone ape? A tide of panic had begun to rise in the household, hushed words were spoken, and then less hushed words. Open accusations:

'That murdering ape ...'

Mr Sallow tried to consider the facts dispassionately. The bodies of two persons, and one cat, had been found in the cellar – all three apparently perfectly healthy apart from being dead. Not likely to be a coincidence. Rivalries within the household might furnish a motive for human murder – but the kitchen cat? It was difficult to see what the three might have in common. And yet, Mr Sallow felt in his bones that they had been killed by the same hand, and popular opinion thought that hand might belong to Crowfoot. Mr Sallow feared a lynching party. Would they have to run away, just when things were going so well here? He was about to head for the cellar once more, in the hopes of finding a helpful trace when the kitchen maid arrived with a message. Crowfoot had been found unconscious and possibly dead, on the cellar floor.

Many ideas, each one more alarming than the last, flitted through Mr Sallow's head as he ran to Crowfoot's side.

Had the household indulged in a summary execution? He'd kill the lot of them.

Or had Crowfoot tried to kill himself?

He was a creature very sensitive to atmospheres, but Mr Sallow didn't think he would understand enough to do such a thing.

The ape lay on the cold flagstones, feet in the air in perfect imitation of the late cat, and in just the same spot.

'What have you done to him?' cried Mr Sallow in great distress.

'We done nothing at all, sir,' said the maid, arms folded. 'This is how he was found.' Mr Sallow knelt by Crowfoot and lifted him tenderly onto his lap. The smell of wine was unmistakable. He listened carefully for the ape's heartbeat, and there it was, a little faint, a little unsteady, but still there.

'I will take care of him,' said Mr Sallow.

'There is nothing more to see. Off you go, all of you.' He glared round and the household dispersed.

As he carried Crowfoot out, the widow appeared before him.

'I told you to keep that creature away from my late husband's wine.' Mr Sallow opened his mouth to reply, but she got in first. 'No, no, don't you dare deny it. I can smell it from here. And look at the state of him!' She wrinkled her nose.

The ape was deeply unconscious, his face stretched into an ugly grin. Guilty as charged. There was nothing Mr Sallow could do but bow and get Crowfoot out of sight.

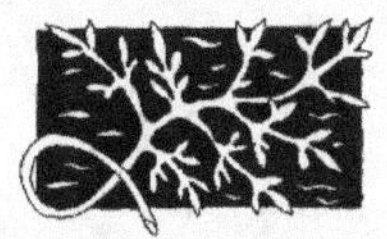

Bitter Buttons

Inspired by the Tansy (*Tanacetum vulgare*), a plant said to symbolise hostility. Another name for it is bitter buttons.

'Poor Crowfoot,' said Mr Sallow. 'He drank wine out of sheer fear. He is a martyr to the drink, poor sensitive creature, at the best of times. But the suspicion that fell upon him has tipped him over the edge.' He was talking to Master Buttons the under-gardener. 'And you, my dear young sir, are the cause of it.' He said this sadly, and not at all unkindly, so the lad bristled a lot less than he might have.

'But I saw him! The butler was on the floor, dead as a doornail, and I saw your ape, I did.'

Mr Sallow looked at the boy thoughtfully.

'What you said at the time, my dear, before many witnesses, was that you saw a shadow on the wall.'

'That's right,' said the boy, after a confused pause, 'I did. But it had prodigious long arms. And who has arms like that, round here? Your ape, that's who.'

Mr Sallow nodded good-naturedly.

'That is true. But if I could prove to you that you were mistaken?'

'You can't,' said the boy, defensively. 'I know what I saw. You're making excuses for that Crowtoes creature.'

'Crowfoot,' said Mr Sallow, softly. 'He's called Crowfoot.'

'Well, whatever he's called, I saw his shadow, and you shan't talk me out of it.'

'Quite right,' said Mr Sallow. 'I shan't. But maybe I can show you with your own eyes that you were mistaken. Come, it won't take long.' And with that he led the boy round to the wine cellar window.

'Now then,' said Mr Sallow. 'You saw the shadow through this window, yes? And it was at this time of day was it not?'

The boy nodded; suspicion written all over his face. He was not about to be swindled out of his moment of glory as Crowfoot's accuser, not if he could help it.

'Just so,' said Mr Sallow. 'Now stand at the window just as you did. What do you see?'

The boy positioned himself at the window and looked.

'Oh!'

Mr Sallow stood back.

'Do you by chance see a long-armed shadow? Raise your right arm if you please. Does the shadow not raise its arm?'

'But I don't have long arms!' spluttered the boy.

'It is a trick of the light, I think, when the sun is at this angle. Look, I shall stand in the same place, and there is another long-armed shadow. What you saw, young sir, was your own shadow, a little distorted by the irregular shape of the wall it falls upon. Nothing fearsome, nor magical. And nothing at all apelike.'

'But ...' said the boy, doubtfully. He was picturing the clip round the ear he was likely to receive for telling slanderous fibs.

Mr Sallow read his mind.

'I shall tell Mistress Cicely that it was an honest mistake on your part. I will bring her, and anyone else who doubts it, down here tomorrow and show them their own long-armed shadows, if need be. You need not fear punishment.'

And so, Crowfoot the Ape was absolved of wrongdoing – apart from helping himself to the late master's wine – and Master Buttons, still slightly stunned at the lack of punishment, became Mr Sallow's most devoted supporter.

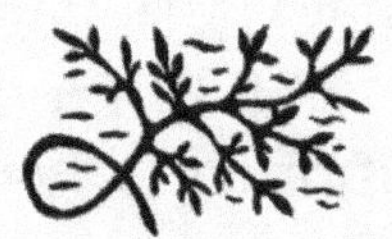

Old Skullcap

Inspired by the Common Skullcap (*Scutellaria galericulata*), a plant that skulks near the waterline.

'Tell me,' Mr Sallow asked Master Buttons, 'at what time of year did the late master die?'

The boy thought a moment. He wasn't the brightest of sparks, Mr Sallow thought, but he would surely know the answer to this.

'In the summertime, sir.'

Mr Sallow nodded.

'And the master before him?'

The boy was defeated.

''fore I was born,' he said. 'You should ask Old Skullcap, sir.'

'And who is he?'

'Don't ye know?' said the boy scornfully. Surely everyone knew Old Skullcap! 'He's a very ancient object what lives by the river. Downstream. And he knows all the histories of hereabouts.'

It seemed that Old Skullcap came from a long line of Skullcaps down the ages, and that he knew everything worth knowing, if Mr Sallow could only get to him before he expired from sheer weight of knowledge. For the first time ever there was no

Young Skullcap to carry on the family tradition, and when the current incumbent was gone, all that history would likely be gone with him. And given the fellow was so very old, Mr Sallow had better get himself down there smartish before it was too late.

So, Mr Sallow and Crowfoot set off on a quest for information, following the riverbank down to Old Skullcap's unsavoury hovel. The grubby old man, who came out took one look at the ape and declared that no such filthy animal would be permitted indoors. This was a little rich coming from someone of such questionable personal hygiene, but nonetheless Crowfoot was left on the doorstep, fuming at the injustice of it.

'Perhaps you can help us,' said Mr Sallow settling himself in the murky interior. Old Skullcap scowled and grunted in a peculiarly animal way. And to think he wouldn't let poor Crowfoot in, thought Mr Sallow. I suppose he wants paying. He produced a couple of coins.

The old man inspected them closely, and then said,

'What is it you want to know?'

'I want to know about the masters of Dropwort Hall if you please. I have learned that the late master died in the summertime. Can you tell me at what time of year the previous masters died?'

'I can,' said Old Skullcap. 'Time out of mind, while I live. What business is it of yours, then?'

'I'm employed at the hall. And in the light of recent deaths there, it's my job to make enquiries.'

Old Skullcap sniggered.

'Won't do you no good,' he said. 'Place is cursed. Everyone knows.'

'Nonetheless ...' said Mr Sallow, starting to put the coins back in his pocket.

'Let's not be hasty.' Old Skullcap shuffled forward and took the coins. 'Well then. For what it's worth, every last one of 'em died in the summertime, just like this last 'un. But people do, don't they? Plagues and agues – dangerous season. Summer agues it was took the lot of 'em, time out of mind.'

Mr Sallow nodded seriously. 'Is that your true opinion then – disease, not curse?'

'You is a intelligent and knowing gent, sir, I perceive. Between you, me and the doorpost, I reckon the curse is a invention, sir. A excuse for a unhealthy house. N'more than that. No magical curses nor none o' that nonsense. They keeps up that little fiction cos it makes 'em feel special up at the Hall.' Old Skullcap sniffed and sneered. 'Also, it stops people asking too many questions when the people dies, y'see. Oh, they says, that'll be the curse, won't it, and has a bit of a shudder, and they leave it be. You, sir, is a rare bird, to be asking about this. And it's 'bout time the truth were told.'

Despite the obvious good logic of this, Mr Sallow was not easily convinced. There are more things in heaven and earth.

'The question is,' he said, as he and the ape made their way back, 'whether these summertime demises were natural, as the old man says, or whether there is indeed a curse on the house.'

Crowfoot, appeased by the brevity of the visit to Old Skullcap, raised an intelligent eyebrow.

'And furthermore ...' Mr Sallow went on, more to himself than to the ape, '... furthermore, is there anything we can do about a curse if there truly is one? And how do these distressing recent deaths fit in, eh? The curse is on the master of the house, not on the servants. It is all very perplexing.'

Crowfoot frowned, clearly wondering if this rather elastic curse might stretch as far as himself. Mr Sallow read his thoughts.

'I truly don't know if you and I are safe, old friend,' he said candidly. The ape climbed up onto his back and clung on resolutely. 'Don't worry, Crowfoot, I have a few theories to explore yet.'

Crowfoot looked as if he'd prefer to forget the whole thing and move on to somewhere safer. But Mr Sallow dashed his hopes.

'There is a presence at Dropwort Hall – animal, vegetable, or mineral – I know not which, but I mean to find out what it is, and how it works.'

The ape clamped a despairing hand over his eyes, apparently thinking that Mr Sallow's inquisitiveness could be the death of the pair of them.

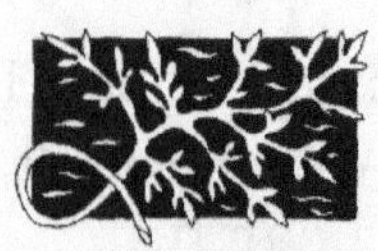

A Drop of Water

Inspired by the Greater Spearwort also called Tongue-leaved Spearwort (*Ranunculus lingua*).

'The wine cellar was the lowest point in the house, but it wasn't fully underground. It was quite well-lit, too, by a couple of little windows. Mr Sallow had ordered the door chained and locked following Crowfoot's indisposition. He had no idea who or what was responsible for this chain of events, of whether they might be deliberately achieved or mere accident, but they all had the cellar in common, so it seemed wise to keep people out, and Crowfoot in particular. Nevertheless, he let himself in to look around and consider the possibilities. If this room only had the power of speech! A few words of whatever tongue it might speak would explain so much, but the room had nothing to say. Mr Sallow sighed and engaged his brain instead. Was it really something to do with the wine, he wondered, however affronted the widow might be at the suggestion? The butler had been found in a puddle of it, the cook had a ladleful in her hand, the cat reeked of it, and Crowfoot had been helping himself.

Mr Sallow chose a bottle at random, opened it, sniffed it, and drank a careful mouthful. Better to experiment on myself than on anyone else, he thought. After a few breathless and fretful minutes, he concluded that it was very good wine indeed. Fruity, full-flavoured, and quite unadulterated. Mr Sallow trusted his own palate in these matters. And what's more he was showing no signs whatsoever of dropping dead. There was nothing at all wrong with this superb wine, and he could only admire the late master's good taste.

While he was considering all this Mr Sallow became aware of a noise. A distinctly out-of-place noise. Faint. Distant. But regular. It sounded like water trickling. He listened intently. Now where was that coming from? He couldn't make it out at all. Was it significant? He didn't know.

The only person that might, was that fount of knowledge on all things Dropwort Hall, Old Skullcap.

So, Mr Sallow collected Crowfoot –nonsense, the fresh air will do you good, my dear– and set off downstream for Old Skullcap's hovel once again.

Mr Sallow got straight to the point:

'Why can I hear water running in the wine cellar?'

Old Skullcap looked at him in silence, waiting, until a coin was placed in his grubby hand.

'Ah,' he said, 'that'll be the old well. It were a fancy scheme. Long time ago now. Drained water from the marshes through a pipe.'

'They don't use it now?' asked Mr Sallow. Crowfoot had refused to come in and was waiting outside the door making huffing noises, with tightly folded arms and a martyred expression.

'No,' said Old Skullcap, glancing at the ape in the doorway and grunting with intense disapproval. 'No. Too unreliable. Leaky pipe. Too much trouble for 'em to upkeep it. They dug a deeper well outside the kitchen door instead. I 'spect the water still trickles through the old pipe now and then, though. No great mystery to that, at all.' He sniffed.

Mr Sallow and Crowfoot, still griping, headed back. Could an unused well have any bearing on the case? Or was it simply another distraction, like the wine? But Mr Sallow liked to be thorough, and he and Crowfoot returned to the wine cellar, the ape keeping a safe distance between himself and the wine bottles.

'There's nothing wrong with it, Crowfoot. I tried it myself. It's your own fault for over-indulging.' Crowfoot looked sheepish.

It took a while to uncover the lost well. An oak lid set into the flagstones was finally found hidden under an empty barrel. The rusted iron ring at its centre, once prised free, offered a way in. Mr Sallow leaned over and peered down. No doubt about it, this was the source of the noise. A very ripe, green, very unappetising smell rose up with the trickling sounds. Crowfoot put his hand over his eyes and hooted.

'This is too much for a delicate stomach, Crowfoot,' said Mr Sallow.

'Go and lie down.' The ape was out of the cellar in a heartbeat.

Dangling from the well-head was a rope and leather bucket. Both were perfectly serviceable. 'Someone,' said Mr Sallow to himself, 'has seen fit to furnish a new set, and not so long ago, either. Now why would anyone bother to do that, I wonder?' Mr Sallow lowered the bucket.

It had been a wet summer, Mr Sallow thought, as he hauled up the bucket, and that probably explained the steady trickle of water into the bottom of the well. It was ingenious, this idea of indoor running water – a thought he put aside for further consideration later – but for now he needed to concentrate. The bucket came up wet and gleaming but contained only a small quantity of water. It was an idea that needed refinement. The water was a deep mossy green, not at all wholesome. Mr Sallow could see why the well had been abandoned. It certainly didn't produce anything drinkable. He poured a little into a jug, so he could take it outside and examine it in daylight. However, he felt this line of enquiry was most likely a blind alley. The water might be tainted – but no-one would choose to drink it. Even the kitchen cat would have had the sense to turn up its nose. So not a very likely murder weapon, really.

Walls have Ears

Inspired by the Water Figwort (*Scrophularia auriculata*), a common waterside plant. The Latin name means 'having ears', because of the ear-like projections on the leaf-bases.

Mr Sallow sensed, all the time, that the house was listening, taking more than a casual interest in whatever might be going on. When he shared this notion with Mistress Cicely the widow, she dismissed it out of hand. She had lived there ever since she was a young bride, and in all those years, had never thought for a moment that the house might be listening.

Houses couldn't listen, could they?

Mr Sallow must be losing his reason if he thought otherwise.

He had bowed and dropped the subject smartly, but had explored it later with Crowfoot, who was a safer confidant.

'Do you not feel it, old friend? The house eavesdropping?' Crowfoot put his hands over his ears. Hear no evil. But he looked fearfully out of the stable window at the bulk of the building in its little park and whimpered.

Mr Sallow went on,

'It's nothing truly malevolent, I don't think. More of an unforgiving nature; a sort of knowingness. The house considers what is for its own good, I think. But I'd rather it didn't know what I might be thinking. Gets in the way.' He looked at the unhappy ape and frowned. 'Hmm. I think we will hold any future discussions outside the house in future. Just to be on the safe side, eh?' Crowfoot nodded. The more time spent out of the house the better, so far as he was concerned.

Willowstrife

Inspired by Purple Loosestrife
or Willowstrife (*Lythrum
salicaria*), a plant said to
encourage psychic powers.

The widow Mistress
Cicely was losing her patience.
Dropwort Hall was alive with
contradictory theories, and
more to the point, there was too
much gossip, and not enough
work being done. The village
constable had declared it was
the curse at work and refused
point blank to have anything
more to do with it.

'There is no need to panic,'
said Mr Sallow.

'No need to panic. People have died!'

'Indeed,' said Mr Sallow, 'and panicking will
not change that. I will find out what has happened,
I promise.'

Even Crowfoot seemed far from happy to be
out and about.

'He thinks that people wish evil upon him,'
explained Mr Sallow. 'It has brought about a
depression. He will recover.'

The idea of a depressed ape in their midst did
nothing to improve anybody's mood, but Crowfoot
did recover, as Mr Sallow said, though he remained

understandably wary. He seemed happier when a journey into the forest to visit the seer was announced. Anywhere, it seemed, would be better than Dropwort Hall, and Crowfoot became visibly more cheerful as Mr Sallow prepared to leave.

Mr Sallow pretended to no magical powers himself – but he had heard tell of a woman of the woods who could solve all conundrums and puzzles. And that, he thought, is just what we need; an outsider, someone with no axe to grind at all, and who might provide a clue, as to what on earth is going on.

'A week away will do you good, too,' said Mr Sallow, affectionately, 'won't it, Crowfoot my dear?'

Crowfoot appeared in favour of the visit and anxious to get on with it.

So, Mr Sallow, with Crowfoot happily packed on his back, set out into the forest to consult with the wise woman he had heard of, convinced she would shed some light on the darkness enveloping Dropwort Hall.

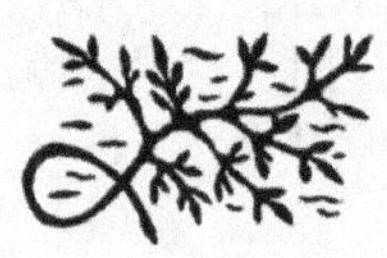

Mistress Osmunda

Inspired by the Royal Fern
(*Osmunda regalis*), a stately
plant favouring in damp
places.

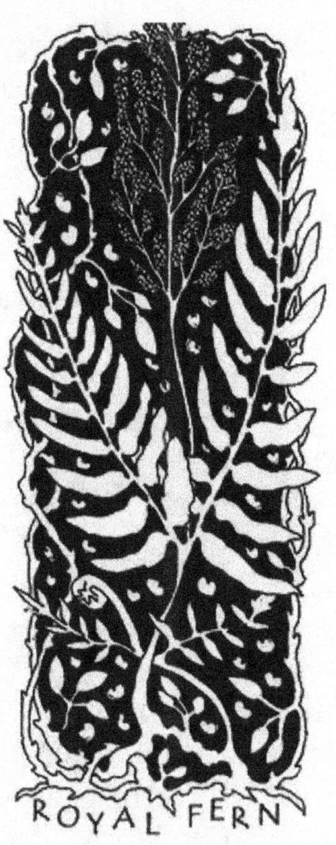

The wise woman, to Mr
Sallow's surprise, turned to be
no more than a girl, and he
wondered just how much
wisdom she had had time to
accumulate.

Crowfoot seemed to see
her as a protective angel, and
went straight to her side,
slipping his hand into hers. Far
too trusting, thought, Mr
Sallow, but he let it lie.

She listened to the whole story attentively,
occasionally asking pertinent questions, and
nodding gravely at the answers.

'So, what do you think?' asked Mr Sallow when
he had finished. 'Murder or misadventure?'

'I will cast the runes,' said the girl, 'they
generally get to the bottom of such questions.'

She turned away from him, working in silence,
for an entranced few minutes. Mr Sallow craned his
neck to see the runes, but she moved to obstruct his
view. Trade secrets, he supposed.

At last, she faced him.

'It is a matter of ancient history.'

51

'Oh, you mean the curse. It is well-known.'

'Possibly. But you have asked the wrong question, master. Ask rather is it greed or rank stupidity and you will get a better answer. Go home, and the solution will be in front of your eyes, if only you can see it.'

Mr Sallow wasn't sure if this made matters clearer or not.

She regarded his puzzled face.

'In this matter, begin in the marsh, not the meadow.'

'Well,' said Mr Sallow, as they journeyed back from their visit to the wise woman, 'there is no getting straight sense out of these seers, is there? She knows the answer to the mystery, I'm sure of it – but can she just tell us so? No, she can't. She has to drop hints and be mysterious.' He stamped his foot in frustration, quite unlike his normal self. 'So now I have to puzzle it out myself.'

Crowfoot the Ape, riding happily on his master's back, had gone to sleep, but the stamped foot shook him awake. The even-tempered, patient, unflappable Mr Sallow was exhibiting signs of a strop. It was a new experience for Crowfoot.

Mr Sallow's mood did not improve greatly when they arrived back at Dropwort Hall. He spent many hours alone gazing out over the marshy area by the river. After three days of silent contemplation, to the concern of everyone in general, but poor Crowfoot in particular, Mr Sallow still stood rooted to the spot, still thinking it through. The solution is in front of your eyes, the wise woman had said; begin in the marsh, not the meadow. He repeated the words over and over to himself until they ceased to have meaning. Marsh and meadow. Meadow and marsh.

What do these two places have in common, and what distinguishes them?

Well, thought Mr Sallow, they are distinguished by the abundance of water, or the lack of it.

What have they in common, though?

He stared intently again at the lush summer plants of the marshland and began to name them to himself. Loosestrife and reed mace, yellow flag, and bur-reed – none of them to be seen in a dry meadow. And then his eye fell upon the most abundant and lush of them all, and his mind began to turn it over and over.

'Well, well,' he said at last. 'What's in a name?' All his suspicions began to make sense, and for the first time in a long while he smiled. Crowfoot, watching from a distance, noticed the change of expression, the move from dark to light, and crept over to take Mr Sallow's hand and look enquiringly up into his face.

'I have it, Crowfoot my dear,' said Mr Sallow. 'Or, at least, I think I have some of it!'

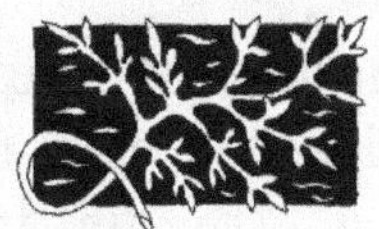

What the Butler Did

Inspired by the Yellow Flag (*Iris pseudacorus*) a plant of watersides and damp places. It was sometimes hung above doors to ward off evil.

'Butler,' said the man on the doorstep, warily. 'Would like a word with ...'

A quick look had told Mr Sallow a great deal. Muddy boots. He had come through the marshes.

Not the way most people approached Dropwort Hall. A wee bit suspicious. And anybody local would have known of the butler's demise. It was the talk of the village. Yet the fellow had turned up on the doorstep expecting to talk with the butler. Most interesting.

'Butler's been detained,' said Mr Sallow, smiling. 'Left me in charge,' he added with a knowing wink.

The man seemed uncertain whether he should press on or run for it. 'Expecting something nasty?' he asked, glancing at the wilting bunch of yellow flags someone had hung in the doorway.

'Superstitious nonsense,' said Mr Sallow, dismissively. 'Come in and have a cup of wine.'

'No,' said the man, 'no, but thank you kindly. I'll just take the consignment, shall I? If you'll watch the door?'

'Help yourself,' said Mr Sallow, standing back and hoping he was saying the right things.

'Ones on the right, as usual?' The man pointed to the wine rack, and Mr Sallow nodded.

Half a dozen of the late master's bottles of finest burgundy were soon neatly stowed in a sack.

'Just a few at a time,' said the man, hoisting the package onto his back. 'Gently does it, eh? Here you are.' And he handed over some coins. 'See you next month.'

And with that he loped out of the door, clinking, and vanished. Mr Sallow looked at the six empty spaces on the wine rack, and then at the coins in his hand, thinking hard. So, the butler had been up to something: selling off the late master's wine to a third party, on a regular basis. A common-enough money-making scheme among servants. The coins, did not add up to the full market value of that exquisite wine, or anywhere near – but that was to be expected, in a no-questions-asked transaction, wasn't it? Mr Sallow had the feeling there was something more, something he was missing, that would explain the butler's death. He sat down to think through everything he had discovered so far, in the hope of piecing it all together.

Mr Sallow recounted the tale of the man and the wine bottles to Crowfoot the Ape. He was the perfect companion, listening intently, and interrupting not at all.

'What bothers me, when I consider it, is why the butler – who, by definition, knows about wines, would sell it quite so cheaply. It is superb – I tasted it myself.'

Crowfoot, who had tasted quite a lot of it, nodded in agreement. Mr Sallow stared into the distance for a moment, and then said,

'But the wine made you very ill, did it not?'

Crowfoot put his hands over his mouth at the memory.

'There was something wrong with it! Or, at least, some of it. That's why he sold it off cheap. It was adulterated.'

Had the butler been selling adulterated wine? And had retribution been visited upon him by his customers?

That might explain the murder. But no – that man had come back for more. Not something a murderer would do. Stranger and stranger.

'I am still missing something, Crowfoot, dear,' said Mr Sallow, 'though I feel I am close. I will go back to the wine cellar and go over it all again.'

Crowfoot made a face which clearly stated that he would give it a miss if it were all the same to Mr Sallow.

Murder times Three?

Inspired by the Trifid Bur-Marigold (*Bidens tripartita*), a waterside herb whose leaves are divided into threes.

'We must gather outside,' said Mr Sallow, 'so the house cannot hear us.'

The widow rolled her eyes but led her household out through the porch as instructed, where they assembled around Mr Sallow, Crowfoot the Ape at his side.

Mr Sallow raised his hands for silence. He bowed to Mistress Cicely.

'With your permission, ma'am, I shall tell everyone what I have discovered. To begin, I regret to inform you that your butler was a thief.'

'And a drunk!' piped up the stable boy. The widow glared at him. 'Well, he was!'

Mr Sallow ignored the interruption.

'He was selling off your late husband's excellent wine, a little at a time.'

'He did what?' cried the widow in outrage.

'By the half dozen. Never fear, ma'am – I have found the agent who was receiving them, and I shall nab him when he returns for the next batch. Justice will be served.'

'Justice cannot be served to my butler,' observed the widow, 'since the villain is already dead.'

'None o' this tells us who the murderer is.' This was the stable boy again, speaking for everyone.

'Just so,' said Mr Sallow. 'But there is more. Not only was he selling the wine, he was adulterating it first.'

'Adulterating?' said the widow, aghast, convinced this was something very ungodly, and ever mindful of her reputation. 'What do you mean?'

'I mean, ma'am, that he was mixing it with water.'

'And then drank the rest himself!' said the stable boy. 'N'wonder he were always drunk!'

'How do you know this, Mr Sallow?' asked the widow.

'Because, ma'am, I discovered the very convenient disused well in the cellar, equipped with new rope and bucket. He could lock the door and water the wine in perfect seclusion, unobserved. I also discovered his system of marking the watered bottles. He had quite a few ready prepared.'

'Perfidious!' said the widow. 'He helped himself to his master's wine and was paid for the privilege too. But how came, he to be dead, then? Did the agent discover what he was about and take retribution?

'I think not,' said Mr Sallow. 'I believe that, in his cups, he confused the bottles and drank from one that had been watered. I kept the fragments, you see, of the one he had in his hand, and it carried his mark. Adulterated.'

'I wish you wouldn't keep saying that' said the widow, crossly. 'In any case, no-one ever died of watered wine, did they? It is reckoned to be health-giving.'

'In general, it is,' said Mr Sallow. 'But this water comes not from your perfectly healthy well, it comes through an ancient system of pipes from the marsh.' This was said as if it explained everything, which it didn't.

The widow tapped her foot impatiently.

'And?'

'Well, ma'am,' Mr Sallow refused to be rushed, 'have you ever considered the naming of this house? No? Allow me to explain. I had thought that it took its name from the dropwort, that very wholesome and scented herb of the grassy meadows. But there is another dropwort, one that haunts the marshes. The water dropwort, also called hemlock, water dropwort, and with good reason, as it is a very venomous herb in all its parts. And there is a vast deal of it in the marshy part of your estate, ma'am. I fear that particular water source in the cellar is contaminated, at least in the summertime, with its poisons. Thus, the butler, by confusing the bottles and drinking this contaminant, was responsible for his own demise.'

'But what about the cook and the cat?' asked the stable boy, before anyone else could get a word in.

'I cannot prove it,' said Mr Sallow, 'but I suspect the cook was also in the habit of helping herself to the wine, and chose the wrong bottle, and the cat, sadly, drank the spillage. So, it is my belief there has been no murder at all, merely degrees of theft and misadventure. The wine will be destroyed, the contaminated well infilled, and there should be no more danger to life and limb in Dropwort Hall than could normally be expected.'

'But it's cursed, Dropwort Hall is!' said the stable-boy. 'That's a danger to life 'n' limb, ain't it?'

'I was coming to that,' said Mr Sallow.

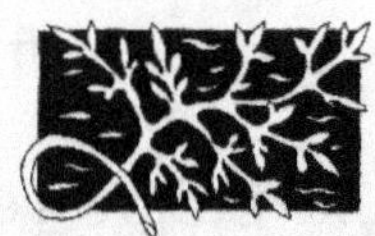

The Curse of Meaningless Words

Inspired by the Hemlock Water Dropwort (*Oenanthe crocata*). Very common in damp places, and very poisonous.

'I have set this house to rights for you,' said Mr Sallow solemnly. 'I have solved conundrums. I have freed you all from suspicion of murder.' Everyone stood in silence. 'No mean feat,' added Mr Sallow, a little self-congratulatory. 'And now I have a final gift for you. I shall lift the curse of Dropwort Hall.'

'There is no curse,' said the widow. Her husband had stubbornly refused all mention of it, until he was mortally stricken with an ague.

He had exclaimed." Well, bless my soul, perhaps there is something in it after all", and expired. She had put this down to sickness rather than sense.

'You proved to us the cause of the recent deaths, all perfectly rational,' she said to Mr Sallow. 'There is no curse.'

'Then you are the only person, ma'am, begging your pardon, who thinks so.' The household nodded as one.

'The curse were passed down through the years, owner to owner,' said the under-gardener. 'Right down to the late master. Everyone knows it.'

Mistress Cicely folded her arms.

'Very well, Mr Sallow, if you must, proceed with this pantomime.'

Mr Sallow ignored the barb and said graciously,

'I thank you, ma'am, and so will the house.' The ape, looking up into his face, pulled on his sleeve.

'Run along, Crowfoot, dear, I'm busy.' The ape fled. 'Now then, during my recent investigations I was able to research the matter a little, and I have discovered an ancient writing which spells it out in some detail.' He took out a piece of parchment and waved it for all to see. 'It stems from an unfortunate argument long ago – a dispute over the ownership of the house. The loser cursed the winner. It is sorcery, I fear, but not indestructible.' The widow snorted, but everyone else took a step backwards. 'It is called the Curse of Meaningless Words.'

The widow snorted again. She simply couldn't help herself. He was making it up, she thought, giving a performance. Well, let him. But she was not about to be taken in like the rest of these gaping fools.

Mr Sallow looked intently at the faces around him.

'This curse can be lifted, oh yes. But there is a slight snag.'

The widow restrained herself from giving another snort. She had just known there would be a difficulty.

Can't make things too easy, can he? So there has to be a snag.

'What is this difficulty, Mr Sallow?' she said impatiently. She was in the middle of working the fiddly bit on an embroidery, and this was a waste of good daylight.

Mr Sallow bowed.

'The difficulty is, ma'am, that lifting the curse requires a sacrifice.'

Everyone took another step back.

'What sort of sacrifice, Mr Sallow? Money, I suppose?' The widow folded her arms more tightly. If he were using this as an opportunity to line his own pockets...

'To be honest, ma'am, it's unclear. But I suspect the sorcerer, however long he may have been dead, will claim one of us to be his servant. Even dead magicians require staff, you know.'

Everyone except the widow looked inclined to run for it.

'Stay where you are!' she said. 'Nothing is going to happen. Let's get this nonsense over with, Mr Sallow.'

'It won't take long, ma'am. I will read the Curse of Meaningless Words aloud – that's all – and it will be broken.'

'So will one of us!' protested the footman.

'Rubbish,' said the widow. 'Proceed, Mr Sallow.'

Mr Sallow read. The widow really couldn't prevent another snort of derision. It was certainly meaningless. Gibberish. He's just making it up, she thought. But you had to admire the sheer nerve of the fellow, reciting rubbish out here when he could be fixing the kitchen chimney. But she closed her eyes and kept quiet until he finished.

Maybe they will believe it and stop fussing about curses. Perhaps that's his intention, after all. Let him finish.

When Mr Sallow fell silent, the widow opened first one eye, then the other, and checked her household. All present and correct.

'There,' she said, 'no-one injured, no-one missing, no curse, no sacrifice required. Now can we get on please? The kitchen chimney is smoking again, and it won't fix itself.'

But Mr Sallow wasn't listening. He was staring wide-eyed at something.

'Oh,' he said. 'Oh.'

Above the arch of the porch door, where he had nimbly clambered to get a good view of proceedings, was Crowfoot the Ape. He had been turned entirely to stone.

Nobody knew whether to be relieved at poor Crowfoot's fate or even more worried than before.

'Oh,' said the stable boy, 'it's all true. The sorcerer has taken the ape for his servant!'

'The curse is lifted, then,' somebody added. 'A cheer for Mr Sallow!'

They cheered, but not very enthusiastically – after all, Mr Sallow had lost his companion. Crowfoot had not always been popular, but this was a heavy price to pay, everyone knew.

Mr Sallow shook his head. 'No!' he cried. 'No! You don't understand. There was no sorcerer. Of course, not ... I made it all up ... I never believed in the curse ... I thought that if I went through the motions, you would all stop believing in it, too, and then I could leave Dropwort Hall a happy house.'

'But you had the curse on a parchment.'

'Yes, but I wrote it myself!'

'But you said there would be a sacrifice.'

'I know, I know. But it isn't real. First thing that came into my head. I needed you to believe it, or the ruse wouldn't work. I investigated the deaths – all quite accidental. I investigated the curse – consulted with Old Skullcap and the Wise Woman as you know – and having thought it through I agreed with them. There was no curse. All the masters of the house died in summertime, of the agues. Made perfect sense. All very logical. But I knew it would take more than a logical argument to put an end to such an entrenched belief, so I pretended I had the means to lift the curse. I made it all up.'

'Is there no way to restore your ape, Mr Sallow?' whispered the widow.

'How can I know?' said Mr Sallow, brokenly. 'I don't know why this has happened. I made it all up ... an invention.'

But as Mr Sallow gazed sadly up at the stone ape, now so much a part of the porch doorway it might always have been there, he thought perhaps he understood. The house had exacted its price for the peace and happiness Mr Sallow wanted for it. He had been guilty of pride and arrogance, convinced he could dispel people's belief in the curse by sheer force of personality. Dropwort Hall had taken it amiss.

'No good deed ever goes unpunished, they say,' murmured Mr Sallow. 'But, oh, Crowfoot my dear, I never thought you would bear the punishment for me.'

Despite the widow's pleas to stay, Mr Sallow soon moved on from Dropwort Hall. It's never a good idea, is it, he thought, as he walked away, to muck about with magic? Or take it lightly? I have learned the hardest of lessons: humility. And he trudged sadly on.

But Crowfoot the Ape, out of necessity, stayed behind. And there he remains to this day, perched on the porch above the door with a look of scandalised surprise on his face.

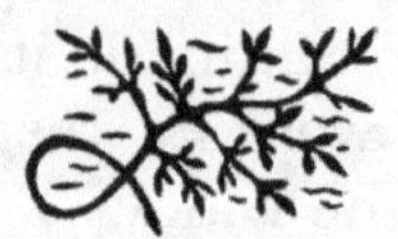

The End

www.ingramcontent.com/pod-product-compliance
Lightning Source LLC
Chambersburg PA
CBHW070511170726
48291CB00008B/2713